SCHOOL BUS
OF HORRORS

UNDER
THE BONNET

BY MICHAEL DAHL

ILLUSTRATED BY EUAN COOK

Raintree
a ... company — publishers for children

Raintree is an imprint of Capstone Global Library Limited, a company incorporated in England and Wales having its registered office at 264 Banbury Road, Oxford, OX2 7DY – Registered company number: 6695582

www.raintree.co.uk
myorders@raintree.co.uk

Designed by Bob Lentz
Original illustrations © Capstone Global Library Limited 2019
Design element: Cover background by Shutterstock: schankz, Nicku
Production by Tori Abraham
Originated by Capstone Global Library Ltd
Printed and bound in India

ISBN 978 1 4747 5933 5
22 21 20 19 18
10 9 8 7 6 5 4 3 2 1

British Library Cataloguing in Publication Data
A full catalogue record for this book is available from the British Library.

CONTENTS

From dawn to dusk, the **SCHOOL BUS OF HORRORS** rumbles along city streets and down country roads, searching for another passenger. Yellow, black markings, dirty windows – it looks like any other school bus.

But **BEWARE!** Step aboard this bus and

experience the scariest ride of your life . . .

CHAPTER ONE
A BAD START

"This is rubbish!" says Aaron, standing in the rain.

He waits without an umbrella at the bus stop.

He puts up his hoodie to keep his hair dry.

A strange bus arrives at Aaron's stop.

It is not the usual bus that takes him to school.

When it slows, the wheels splash water up from the street.

Aaron's face gets soaked. His glasses slide off his nose.

Aaron searches for his glasses on the ground.

CRUNCH!

He steps on the frames.

They split in two.

"Could this day get any worse?"
Aaron asks himself.

CHAPTER TWO
SHADOW SHAPE

Aaron stomps onto the bus, carrying his broken glasses.

He is wet and angry.

He sits down in the front seat. It is the only empty seat left.

The door closes, the engine revs up, and then the bus drives down the street.

Aaron stuffs his broken glasses into his bag. He can hardly see anything without them.

He stares out of the wet windscreen and notices a shadow.

The shadow slinks out from under the bonnet. It sits on the bonnet like a big, black bin bag.

Aaron watches as a thin shape stretches out from the lump.

It looks like an arm. A long, hairy arm!

The end of the arm is shaped like a claw.

Aaron stares.

The shadowy claw seems to be holding a hammer.

"Hey, what is that?" Aaron says.

A sign blinks on above him.

Aaron squints to read it: "DO NOT TALK TO THE DRIVER."

The bus driver sits behind a plastic safety wall.

On the wall is a small opening.

The driver's wrinkled hand pokes through the opening.

The hand points up at the sign.

Aaron keeps staring out of the windscreen.

"Can't you see that?" he says to the plastic wall.

The claw-like hand rises again from the shadowy lump.

Then the arm swings down hard.

BANG! The hammer strikes the bonnet of the bus.

CHAPTER THREE
HAMMER

Aaron screams, and the other passengers stare at him.

"What's your problem?" asks a girl across the aisle.

"Look on the bonnet!" says Aaron.

He grips a nearby pole and stands, still looking out of the window.

The girl across the aisle ignores him.

Aaron pulls one half of his broken glasses from his bag.

He holds the lens up to his eye.

The shadow is clearer now.

It is a creature with long arms and suction feet. Its fur shines in the falling rain.

BANG! BANG!

The hammer hits the bonnet again and again.

CHAPTER FOUR
THE MONSTER

"Can't you hear that?" shouts Aaron.

The sign lights up again: "DO NOT TALK TO THE DRIVER."

As Aaron watches, the creature tears off half of the metal bonnet.

The shadow shape reaches its long arms down under the bonnet.

Sparks fly out from the engine.

Aaron sees the hairy claws pulling long, rubbery wires.

The bus is going to crash! thinks Aaron. *The driver has to stop!*

Aaron jumps up from his seat.

He hurls himself at the plastic wall surrounding the driver.

He shoves his arm through the opening.

Aaron grabs the steering wheel.

"Stop the bus!" he shouts.

The bus comes to a sudden stop.

Aaron stumbles down the stairs and out of the door.

He sees figures walking on the pavements around him.

Many of them hold umbrellas.

"Help!" Aaron shouts. "There's a monster on the bus!"

The figures stop and lower their umbrellas.

They are not human.

They are hairy creatures with long arms and suction feet.

A small creature holding its mother's hand points at Aaron and screams.

"It's a monster!" the mother creature shouts.

Aaron starts to run.

The creatures chase after him, growling angrily.

As Aaron flees, his head slips out from under his hoodie.

His hair is quickly soaked. But now Aaron hardly even notices.

GLOSSARY

aisle walkway that runs between a row of seats

creature living thing, human or animal

lens see-through, curved piece of glass or plastic used in pairs of glasses

revs makes an engine run quickly and noisily

rubbery tough and stretchy, like rubber

suction sticky; suction removes air between objects allowing them to stick together

DISCUSS

1. Why do you think this book is called *Under the Bonnet*?

2. At the beginning of the story, the rain bothered Aaron. At the end, he didn't even notice it. What changed?

3. In chapter one, Aaron says, "Could this day get any worse?" By the end of the story, how do you think he would answer this question? Explain.

WRITE

1. Create a new title for this book. Then write a paragraph about why you chose your new title.

2. Draw a picture of a scary monster. Then give your monster a name and write a story about it.

3. Write about the scariest bus journey you've ever experienced.

AUTHOR

MICHAEL DAHL is the author of the Library of Doom series, the Dragonblood books and Michael Dahl's Really Scary Stories. (He wants everyone to know that last title was not his idea.) He was born a few minutes after midnight of April Fool's Day in a thunderstorm, has survived various tornados and hurricanes, as well as an attack from a rampant bunny at night ("It reared up at me!"). He currently lives in a haunted house and once saw a ghost in his high school. He will never travel on a school bus. These stories will explain why.

ILLUSTRATOR

EUAN COOK is an illustrator from London, who enjoys drawing pictures for books and watching foxes and jays out of his window. He also likes walking around looking at broken brickwork, sooty statues and the weird drainpipes and stuff you can find behind old run-down buildings.

SCHOOL BUS *OF* HORRORS